MY BOOK

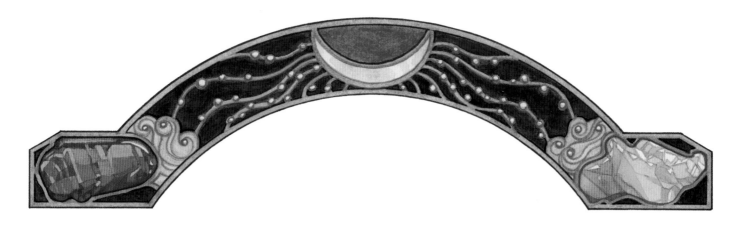

CALIFORNIA
the Magic Island

CALIFORNIA the Magic Island

Doug Hansen

Heyday
Berkeley, California

Dedicated to Keith Hansen
and the magic island of Bolinas, CA

Library of Congress Cataloging-in-Publication Data

Hansen, Doug, author, illustrator.
  California, the magic island / Doug Hansen.
      pages cm
  Summary: Summoned by Queen Calafia to the island of California,
twenty-six animals of the state of California introduce themselves,
their homeland, and the people who dwell there.
  ISBN 978-1-59714-332-5 (hardcover : alk. paper)
  [1. Animals~California~Fiction. 2. California~History~Fiction. 3.
Alphabet.] I. Title.
  PZ7.H198246Cal 2016
  [Fic]~dc23
                          2015015206

Heyday is an independent, nonprofit publisher and unique cultural institution. We promote widespread awareness and celebration of California's many cultures, landscapes, and boundary-breaking ideas. Through our well-crafted books, public events, and innovative outreach programs we are building a vibrant community of readers, writers, and thinkers. To travel further into California, visit us at www.heydaybooks.com.

Cover Art: Doug Hansen
Cover Design: Doug Hansen and Ashley Ingram
Interior Design/Typesetting: Ashley Ingram

Orders, inquiries, and correspondence should be addressed to:
Heyday
P.O. Box 9145, Berkeley, CA 94709
(510) 549-3564, Fax (510) 549-1889
www.heydaybooks.com

Manufactured by Regent Publishing Services, Hong Kong; printed in China

10 9 8 7 6 5 4 3 2 1

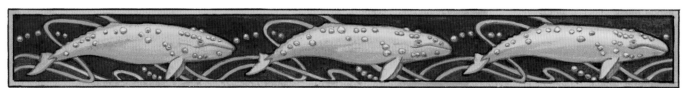

CONTENTS

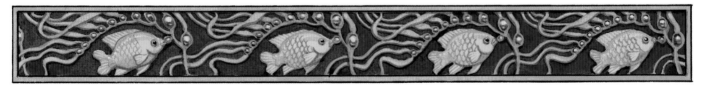

Calafia, Queen of the Magic Island

Queen Calafia and Her Magic Island

Once upon a time (or maybe only yesterday) there was a magic island called California. The ruler of the island was (or still is) a fearless and beautiful queen named Calafia, an unforgettable vision of splendor in her royal robes and golden armor, with shining ornaments blazing in her black hair and pearls glowing against her dark skin.

The magic island is Calafia's kingdom and the home of her warrior women. No men or outsiders are allowed there. The women are like goddesses: stronger, more beautiful, and more skillful than any human. All are confident hunters and expert in capturing and training the wild griffins found there.

If you have never heard of a griffin, imagine a creature with the head and wings of an eagle, but with the body and tail of a lion. Griffins are as ferocious as eagles and as brave as lions. No outsider knows the secret of how the warrior women tame the griffins, or how they ride them on land and through the air.

But riding griffins and hunting are not the only skills of the island women. Some crafted Queen Calafia's sandals and robes; others shaped her jewelry and armor. Calafia generously rewards the women who are expert at building, growing, healing, singing, and charting the stars.

The magic island of California is a paradise. Fruit trees and all kinds of useful plants grow abundantly in the valleys and gardens. Not only griffins but other, more familiar, animals live there too. Calafia is proud of her people and proud to rule an island of such beauty and magic.

This California island paradise is also a natural fortress; the world's wildest cliffs and sharpest rocks surround it. Gold is the only metal found on Queen Calafia's island and the waves splash pearls on the beaches below the cliffs.

Adventurers heard stories of the island of gold and pearls and tried again and again to find it. But no human has ever landed on the island (or even seen it), because it is forever protected by Calafia's

magic. Mists of invisibility hide it from prying eyes. And if explorers come near the island by accident, driven by storms or ocean currents, the griffin riders smash their ships or chase them away. Humans may foolishly include the island on their maps but they can never find it, because California floats wherever Queen Calafia decides it should go.

The Queen's Fury

For centuries California was an island of harmony...until the day Calafia's lieutenant and bodyguard, Liota, brought news of a disturbing discovery.

"Wise and beautiful queen, some upstarts in a distant land have taken to using the name of our magic island. They dare to call their own land 'California.' Surely there can only be one California, not two. Imagine the results of such confusion. What do you command?"

Queen Calafia, always quick to anger, was outraged that her reputation, as well as the legendary name of her fortress paradise, might be dishonored by outsiders. "It is impudence to suggest that any other place on earth can compare with my beloved magic island!" she shouted. "I command that you send my mounted warriors on five hundred griffins to punish those disrespectful 'Californians.' Lay their land to waste and destroy them, just as centuries ago we destroyed the armies of Constantinople."

Calafia's Command

But a great queen must not let anger overrule her wisdom. After a moment, Calafia controlled her fierce temper. "Hold!" she commanded her warriors. "Do not attack...yet.

"Our beloved island of California is a wild land, endowed with magic and favored with rare beauty. We are blessed with abundant gold, diverse creatures, and resourceful people," she declared. "Never did I imagine that any other land might claim to be the equal of mine. Could these foolish people of 'California' be misguided enough to believe they honor us by taking our name?

"However that may be, I must not condemn them until I learn more about their country. But if those aggravating people are brought before me, I will surely lose my temper again...and feed them to the griffins. Besides, our laws decree that no person from outside may ever set foot upon our magic island. Instead, I will summon the wild creatures of this other 'California' to appear before us."

Queen Calafia spoke to her lieutenant. "Liota, I command you to consider any creature that is willing to speak for its homeland. Choose from those that live in the present time, and include creatures from the past as well—even the ancient past. The magic of our island will make that possible. Charge them to speak freely about themselves, and especially to describe their homeland and the people who dwell there.

"My anger is not with these innocent birds and beasts, but everything will depend on the stories they tell. I will judge whether their land and people compare favorably to mine and whether our reputation has been harmed. If I am satisfied, then the people of 'California' will not be punished. My warrior army will not destroy their land. Instead I will honor them with my name and promise to watch over them forever."

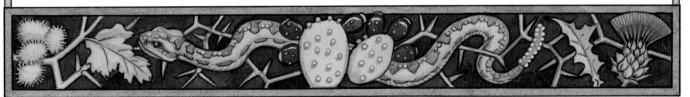

"I hear and obey," said Liota. "Following our customs, no human shall come near our island. Instead we will gather these wild creatures so that we may hear their stories. How many shall we bring before you?"

"One for each finger and toe of my agile limbs," declared Calafia, "one for my nimble tongue, one for my imperishable breath, two for my ears that hear every sound, and two for my far-seeing eyes. Let twenty-six creatures describe to us their 'California,' and bid them speak well."

Without delay, twenty-six griffin riders of the magic island of California flew off and, before long, returned with all of the wild creatures that would speak before the queen.

Everyone assembled in Calafia's royal audience chamber. The spacious, glittering gallery was in a natural cavern, which made the free-tailed bat feel right at home. Birds settled upon whichever perch suited them best. Mammals paced or scuttled self-consciously to their places. Reptiles raised their heads attentively and ocean dwellers quietly rose to the surface of their saltwater pools.

Animals who usually did not get along agreed in whispers that the occasion demanded their best behavior. Out of respect for the queen they would use their finest manners and most polite speech.

The queen sat silently on her throne. Her face showed neither welcome nor anger, only a very solemn expression.

When the time came for each animal to speak, Liota escorted it to the foot of Calafia's throne.

The Doomed Explorer of Alta California

"All-seeing Queen Calafia, I am called Wit, the condor. The animals chose me to speak first because I do not fear your anger."

"Then continue, fearless condor," said the queen.

"Like your griffins, I soar high on broad wings. My keen eyes follow everything that moves and struggles below. From wolf to whale, every creature that dies belongs to me.

"I was the first to spy the men who angered you by naming this land Alta California. It was hundreds of years ago. They were sailors and soldiers aboard wooden sailing ships. The legend of your beauty and your riches lured them, and they believed they had discovered your island. They traded and talked with the native people, always asking where to find the gold and pearls.

"Their leader called himself Cabrillo. He was a fearless explorer. One day he slipped from a boat, splintering his shinbone. I watched that wounded man as I would watch any wounded animal. After many days he died. His crew buried him on an island, but it wasn't your magic island. The men sailed away, but I tell you they will come back again, searching for gold and glory."

"They were courageous and adventurous...and foolish to chase a legend," responded Calafia.

Journey of a Monarch Butterfly Queen

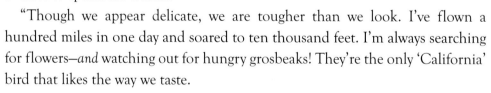

"Graceful Queen Calafia, I too am a queen: Dana the monarch butterfly, royalty in the world of butterfly beauty.

"I started as a hungry caterpillar, hatching from a tiny egg on a milkweed plant, and then became a pupa. Inside my chrysalis I metamorphosed into a butterfly. In autumn I emerged and first spread my wings. Somehow I *knew* that our 'California' would be a magic land for monarchs. I left the northern cold and migrated to a special grove of trees to spend the winter.

"Though we appear delicate, we are tougher than we look. I've flown a hundred miles in one day and soared to ten thousand feet. I'm always searching for flowers—*and* watching out for hungry grosbeaks! They're the only 'California' bird that likes the way we taste.

"One sunny spring day I'll do my spiral mating flight and begin my final journey. I'll search for milkweed plants and lay my eggs. By summer I'll be weary and worn, but my beautiful offspring will flutter away, throughout the north and west. Next autumn, some of my monarch great-great-grandchildren will return to rest in this very grove."

"Fellow queen," said Calafia, "I honor your endurance and perseverance."

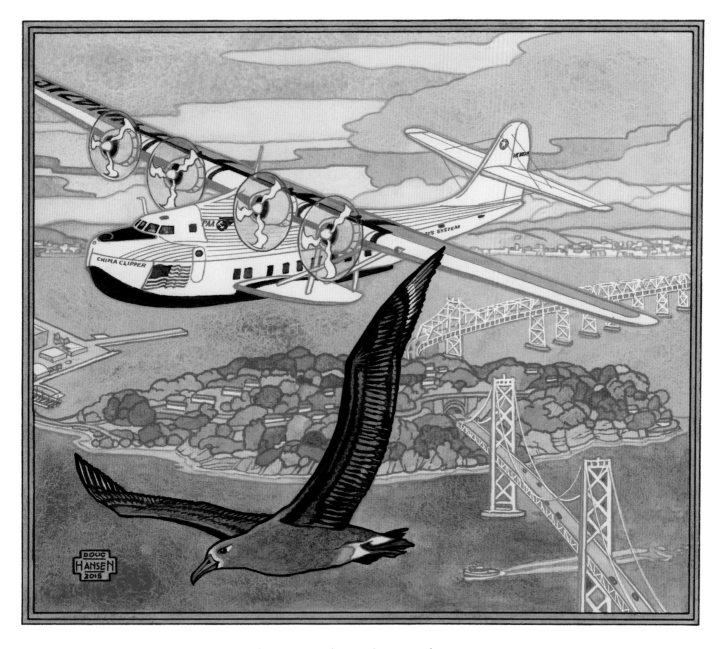

Chasing the *China Clipper*

"Oh Queen Calafia, mistress of the western ocean, I am Black-foot, the albatross. Once in my ocean travels I spied your magic island but I promise I'll never reveal where.

"I was hatched on the beach at tiny Wake Island, and that's where I first saw the seaplane named *China Clipper*, in 1940. It didn't need runways for takeoff and landing. It could float on the ocean just as I do. The airplane's wings were long, and so are mine. Its journey started in China and I've also been to the China Sea. The clipper is a lot like me!

"Curious, I followed the plane eastward as it disappeared toward lonely Midway Atoll. Modern jets can cross the Pacific in one flight but the clipper had to 'island hop' to refuel. Where would it stop next?

"For days I rode the wind currents or floated with my friends to rest and dabble for squid. We sighted the clipper again in a familiar place, the Hawaiian Islands. Soon it took off and so did we, and I was happy when the long journey of the *China Clipper* ended at Treasure Island in San Francisco Bay. Since then I've always been glad to return to my 'California' home."

"You must always keep the location of my island secret," warned Calafia.

The Wild Horses of Death Valley

"Oh Calafia, queen without equal, I am a wild horse, a mustang only two summers old.

"Fierce queen, is your rugged island as beautiful as my forbidding valley? Early travelers named it Death Valley because of the sandstorms and dust devils, and the air so hot that birds fell dead from the bushes. Those travelers didn't know the secrets of survival. For us horses, it is the valley of life.

"No human will ever master us. Our band of wild horses follows the lead mare in single file. We trust her to  guide us to water seeps and saltgrass. Sometimes we must trek all day and night before we eat or drink. For shade, the deep canyons are best, but from the high ridges we can spot predators before they get close.

"Once the rattle of a sidewinder startled me. I bolted and ran—fast and far. The herd stallion chased me back with bumps and bites. 'Never leave the band!' The stallion stays at the rear to protect the mares and foals. When I'm a grown stallion I'll have my own band too."

"Your desolate and savage land is strangely fascinating," murmured the queen.

The Earthquake and the Firehouse Dog

"Hail, Queen Calafia, whose beauty burns bright. I'm a San Francisco firehouse dog with a big story to tell! I guard the fire station and my friends the horses pull the fire engine.

"I'll never forget waking up to the big 1906 earthquake. The ground was rolling like the waves in the bay. Then the earth jerked like a rat shaken by a terrier dog. I barked to warn the horses and firemen. Our wooden firehouse fell down. Brick buildings fell too. Sidewalks cracked. Frightened people in pajamas crowded the streets. Other horses, even cattle, ran madly. Soon, big fires roared high into towers of glowing smoke.

"'*Rowf! Rowf!*' I barked to clear the way and to help the horses run fast. Bystanders chanted, 'Push! Push!' and helped shove the fire engines up steep streets. Firemen used broken doors as heat shields. People beat on flames with mops and sacks, and soldiers even tried to stop fires with dynamite. Sailors took people to safety on boats. After three days and nights of fighting fire, my bark was all gone—but at last, the fire was out. We survived disaster and we'll build again."

Calafia wondered aloud, "Is everyone in your land so determined?"

The Forty-Niners' Gold Rush Scramble

"Oh golden Queen Calafia, may your luster never fade. I am your humble servant, the western gull. I skim the ocean and scavenge the shore for my meals.

"I am always busy where humans are busy. I watch them from the rooftops and docks. I saw the gold seekers coming here from everywhere by ship, by foot, and by wagon. It was the year 1849, so we called them 'forty-niners.'

"In the port of San Francisco there were flocks of ships with sails as white as my feathers. But the sails hung

slack and their bare masts looked like a floating forest. The ships were empty because no sailors were left aboard.

"When gulls gather and cry out '*Cree, cree, cree!*' it means there is food for the taking, and we fight and tangle and grab for it. It's the same with the sailors. When someone cries out 'Gold, gold, gold!' they leave their captains and ships behind, jump into boats, and rush to the goldfields with shovels and picks to scrabble and wrangle and grab for the gold."

"An ugly scramble to secure such beauty," said the queen.

Fall of the Giant Redwoods

"Oh Calafia, queen of mountain, coast, and forest, *'Hup, hoo-hoo, hooo!'* That is the spotted owl salute. My name is Strix. Usually I stay hidden in the broken top of a giant coast redwood tree, watching for prey.

"The redwood trees are the tallest on earth, and some are seven hundred years old. Their bark protects them from insects and fire but not from the axes and saws of the loggers. Cutting up one tree makes enough boards to build many houses. But if they chop down my tree, then where can I go to live?

"Loggers work hard, chopping and sweating and sawing, sometimes for days to cut down one big tree. They make trees fall in the direction they want them to go. *Tim-berrr!* Oxen or little steam engines haul the logs away to sawmills.

"I watched people dance on the stump of one giant tree in the 1850s. I saw a wagon and horses pose for a photograph on a fallen giant. Some men even chopped a tunnel so a carriage could drive through a tree. That's not funny. *Who-hoo-hoo* needs a tree tunnel?"

"Work and play, build and destroy: it's all mixed up in 'California,'" observed the queen.

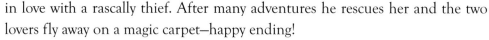

Secrets of Hollywood Movie Magic

"*Rawk!* Ahoy, Queen Calafia, and welcome to Hollywood. *Rawk!* I'm your guide, an Amazon mealy parrot from South America. I'm an animal actor and a stunt parrot. I've appeared in lots of pirate movies. *Rawk*, pieces of eight! That's my favorite line.

"Have I got a story for you, Queenie. Imagine a 1940 movie set in ancient Baghdad. A gorgeous princess falls in love with a rascally thief. After many adventures he rescues her and the two lovers fly away on a magic carpet—happy ending!

"The actors, directors, and extras work hard to make movie magic. Did you notice some of the movie tricks? Thin wires hold up the flying carpet, and a fan makes wind. That fantastic city back there is actually a model. We move the camera up close to make it look big. Workers paint scenery, make wooden swords and other props, and decorate costumes with fake jewels. But believe me, everything looks real in the finished movie. In Hollywood we turn dreams into reality."

"Movie tricks!" exclaimed Queen Calafia. "My griffins fly *without* wires. My sword is made of genuine gold and my royal robes glitter with rare jewels."

"*Rawk*," exclaimed the parrot. "Hollywood can't beat *your* magic!"

14

The Imperial Valley and the Great Flood

"Oh invulnerable Queen Calafia, I am a venomous lizard, a Gila monster. I rarely leave my desert burrow unless I come out to hunt for eggs.

"I used to have a burrow close to the Colorado River, in 'California.' Then some engineers designed a canal to take water from the river for farmers in the Imperial Valley. Before long, river sand clogged the canal.

"So they cut a new channel from the river to the canal, and they were in a hurry. Bad decision! Unexpected rains swelled the river, overflowed the channel, and destroyed its control gates. That's when I abandoned my burrow for good. The rampaging river changed course and followed the canal, cutting away the earth, flooding farms, and eventually pouring into a vast basin called the Salton Sink—but that sink had no drain. It filled up, and half of the Imperial Valley was covered forever by what people now call the Salton Sea.

"For two years, the surging Colorado broke dam after dam. Desperate workers tried to stop the water with huge mats woven from cables and reeds. They dumped trainloads of rock, gravel, and clay from railroad trestles to plug the gap. Finally, in 1907, they forced the river back into its course."

"The 'Californians' wanted running water," joked Calafia. "Instead they got a runaway river."

The Glittering Tower of Jewels

"*Coo-cuk-cuk-cuk-cooo.* Greetings, oh radiant Queen Calafia. A pigeon's life is not easy. No one feeds me. I used to search the streets of North Beach for food scraps and sleep on a window ledge.

"But my life changed when the people of San Francisco built the 'Jewel City' for their 1915 Panama-Pacific world's fair. I chose the Tower of Jewels as my new home. It was covered with shimmering cut-glass gems that swung in the breeze. Emerald, tourmaline, and amethyst matched the green, pink, and purple colors of my feathers. The jewels sparkled in the sun or gleamed at night in the beams of searchlights.

"Every day I visited the Court of Flowers and flew to the Palace of Food Products. I sipped water from the Fountain of Energy and ate spilled café food. Sardine sandwiches, chicken tamales, and chocolate cake were my favorites.

"When the fair ended, everything was torn down—even my Jewel Tower. *Craaash!* I saved one jewel for a souvenir. It was time for me to find *another* new home. I chose the only remaining building...the Palace of Fine Arts. That's where I live now: in a palace!"

"They invent a new world every day in your 'California!'" exclaimed Calafia.

King Sargon's Palace

"Crrroak, crrroak, crrroak! Oh Queen Calafia, Corvus the raven greets you. My raven relatives make their homes everywhere in California—desert, mountain, farm, and city. In my city, Los Angeles, there is a magnificent six-story construction I must tell you about, a king's palace with walls 1,750 feet long. Images of warriors, chariots, and strange-looking figures with four wings decorate the walls. Statues of winged bulls with human heads guard the entrance. When it was built, in 1929, I was afraid to fly over the palace. But we ravens are inquisitive birds and my curiosity overcame my fear."

"I fear no king," remarked Calafia, "and my griffins are a match for anything that walks or flies. Continue your story."

"Yes, fearless queen. What do you think I found behind the palace walls? Four-winged monsters? An army of warriors? Piles of treasure? No, I found a huge tire factory! Thousands of men work there day and night making rubber automobile tires and inner tubes. At sundown when I return to my rocky roost I see the weary men below, blackened by rubber dust, heading for their cars, the highway, and home. They are almost as black as my beautiful feathers."

"I am learning that things in your land aren't always what they appear to be," declared the queen.

Struggle for Survival at the La Brea Tar Pits

"Oh eternal Queen Calafia, pardon me if I speak...slowly. I am the giant ground sloth. I am known for moving... slowly. And why not? The plants and roots that I eat can't run away. Moving quickly can be a...fatal mistake."

"Take your time, mighty sloth," responded Calafia, "A great queen knows the rewards of patience."

The sloth continued. "If you ever visit my home and you get thirsty, watch out for what we call the...'black tar water.' Can you guess why? Because underneath what looks like shining water is...deadly, sticky asphalt...slowly

seeping up from underground. One wrong step and any animal, large or small, may be...trapped in the gummy...ooze, never to escape.

"I saw a frightened mammoth plunge into the asphalt seep. Mammoth is biggest of us all, but he couldn't pull free. Sabretoothed Cat leaped, too quickly, onto Mammoth's neck. Mammoth flung that Sabretooth into the tar pit. Trapped together, they would...perish together! Dire wolves circled the...doomed creatures, trying to finish them off. Teratorns flapped heavily and...waited for the kill."

"Your land is beautiful—and so full of danger," remarked Queen Calafia.

Tale of a Twenty-Mule Team

"*Yip! Yip! Yip!* Oh solitary Queen Calafia, I am Coyote and I honor you. I wander the desert alone and have seen many surprising sights.

"I saw twenty mules pulling heavy wagons loaded with tons of borax rock. It was sometime around 1888. A 'teamster' guided the mule team around a bend and a 'swamper' handled the rear wagon brakes. Two men alone could never move those wagons, but with the mules they can!

"Having a horse for a mother and a donkey for a father means mules are strong and smart. I saw that each mule knew its name and its job.

"Sampson and Gibraltar, the sturdiest mules, were the 'wheelers.' Ahead of them the 'pointers,' Molly and Johnny, steered the wagons. When the teamster called out to Bessie, Baldy, Breezy, and Buttercup, the mules would jump over the long chain to make a tight turn. Next came the five 'swing teams.' Diablo and Brimstone liked teasing Hurricane and Hammerhead, the rawest young mules, but Jasper and Joker, Pancho and Milky, and Zephyr and Cal behaved themselves. They followed the leaders, Prudence and Fancy Dan.

"I'm content to survive on my own, but those mules showed me the power of the team."

"Yes," said the queen. "Cooperation gets the job done."

On Maneuvers with the Navy

"Oh Queen Calafia, I'm Delphina, the dolphin. Your legendary vigor and athletic skills inspire me. I cruise the sunny Pacific with my pod of dolphin friends and family. For exercise we leap high and show off with somersaults and splashes. We stick together in case we run into hungry predators. We can zoom around them or make a defensive circle. When we ram them with our snouts, sharks and orcas leave us alone.

"Once—it was in 1940—we were playing a game called 'bow riding' with a racy little ship. It was painted gray and had many guns: it was a Navy ship. The sailors cheered as we surfed their bow wave. A big warship charged up behind them. Then an even bigger one came churning along—a battleship! A submarine surfaced next to us and patrol boats skimmed past. Flights of Navy airplanes soared overhead in 'V' formations, searching and scouting.

"The Pacific Fleet was practicing defense and attack. The ships turned together and made smoke. Now they were steaming to their home ports with all flags flying. I guess they were showing off too."

"These 'Californians' are mighty at sea," Calafia confided to her lieutenant.

The Observatory and the "Big Eye"

"Oh Queen Calafia, whose glory shines by day and night, hear my story. I am a bird of the species known as the 'common poor-will.' I scoop up insects with my big, wide mouth. Though I nest on the ground, I keep my eyes on the sky: that way I can spot my prey. At dawn and dusk I hunt by the pale light of the moon and stars.

"When I look at the stars they seem to form pictures. I see a squirrel, a moth, and a snake. Glorious queen, what pictures do you see in the stars?"

"Our constellations are the Spear and Shield, the Crown, and the Griffin," answered the queen.

"Have you heard about the 'big eye'?" continued the poor-will. "It isn't really an eye. It is a reflecting telescope with a 200-inch mirror at one end—much bigger than *my* little eyes! Scientists designed it to look deep into space. In the 1930s engineers built a nest for the telescope, an observatory. It's on top of Palomar Mountain, right where I live and hunt. When some clumsy workers widened the mountain road, they ruined my nesting spot. After that, I watched from a safe place as three big tractors, two pushing and one pulling, crept slowly uphill to deliver the big crate containing the precious mirror for the 'big eye.'"

"Curiosity and inventiveness are good qualities," thought Calafia.

A Night Ride with the Pony Express

"Oh swift Calafia, I am Sabrina the flying squirrel. By day I nest high in a dead treetop. I do my flying at night, gliding from tree to tree. While searching for acorns I often see owls, bobcats, and raccoons, but I was startled one night—it was the spring of 1860—when a man suddenly appeared on horseback. He was tearing along like a mule deer with a mountain lion on its tail! Leaves and acorns flew everywhere; pine branches whipped the horse and rider as they skirted boulders and trees.

"Nights later, another horseman came racing through the forest. This time I glided close to get a good look. It was the Pony Express. It's said that nothing—not wolves or warriors, not blizzards or bandits—can stop the Pony Express from delivering the mail.

"The rider was young. He carried a pistol, knife, and rifle. Pockets on his *mochila*—saddle pouch—were just big enough for an armful of letters. He blew a horn to let a relay station know he would soon arrive. When he got there he dismounted and, barely pausing, threw his mochila on a fresh pony and galloped headlong to the next station."

"The people of this other 'California' do their utmost to meet any challenge," the queen said, with admiration.

The Little Lost Quail

"Kindly Queen Calafia, please hear my story. I'm a California quail. My family calls me 'Pillow' because I'm soft and plump. I have six brothers and six sisters in my brood. Mother hatched us and kept us warm when we were chicks. We all walk in an orderly line. Walking is better than flying when you're looking for seeds and sprouts.

"I've already had an adventure. One day I was following a snail...and strayed far away from my brood. Oh queen, I was all alone! Then I remembered that Mother taught me to call 'chi-CAH-go' if I was ever lost. So I called 'chi-CAH-go'...and there was Father on sentinel duty, watching over me. Just then, he gave his warning call, 'pit-pit, pit-pit.' A scary hawk shadow drifted close to me. I scurried for my life. My brothers, sisters, and cousins—all of us—ran faster than you can imagine and then we 'froze' in the protective shadow of a dead tree trunk.

"Later, the covey gathered in a safe and sunny spot. We cleaned our feathers by taking a dust bath (we don't have to undress). Then, as we do every night, my family roosted together, snug and happy."

"Are the human families in 'California' as devoted as yours?" asked Calafia.

Working on the Railroad

"Oh Calafia, you are queen of craggy cliffs and menacing mountains. I am the bighorn sheep, sure-footed with four strong legs. My sharp hooves never slip, and heights don't frighten me. I lived undisturbed in my High Sierra home...until the railroad men came.

I can skip along steep mountains and leap over deep canyons, but how could people on just two legs ever hope to build a track over those towering walls of rock? Surprise! The railroad workers tunneled through the mountains and bridged the chasms with wooden trestles.

"I won't forget the noise of sawing and shouting as trees fell to clear a path; of scraping shovels and cracking picks; of men chanting as they laid timbers and rails. Shouts and curses echoed in English and Irish, Welsh and Chinese. Explosions set off by dynamite rumbled day and night. Broken boulders thundered down.

"It was in 1867 that I heard a train whistle shriek. Men began to cheer. I knew that the first locomotive had cleared the highest tunnel."

"The ingenious people of 'California' conquer even the wild mountains," said the queen.

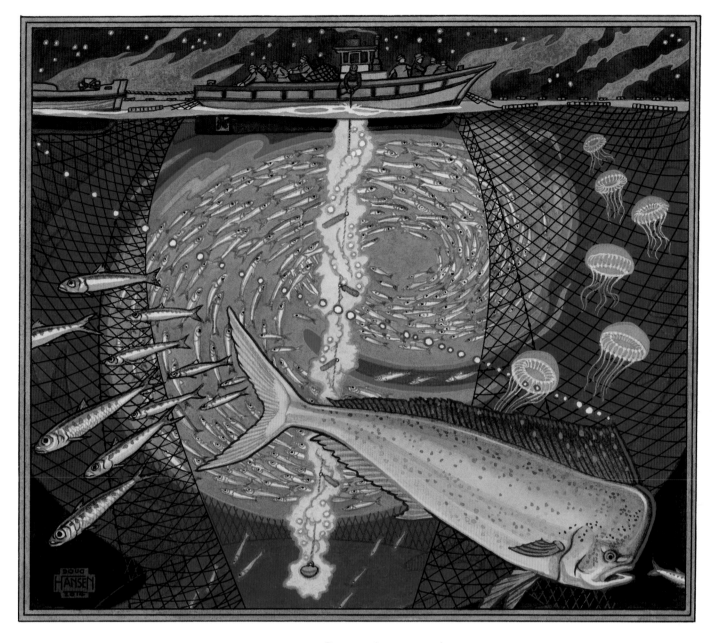

Secrets of Sardine Fishing

"Oh glittering Queen Calafia, I am Cory, the mahi-mahi. Have you ever tasted a slippery little Pacific sardine? Thousands of them gather in swift, swirling schools. Maybe they gather to confuse predators—like me—with so many moving targets. Or maybe each sardine just hopes some other sardine will get eaten. Either way, I always manage to swallow a few.

"One moonless night off Monterey, as I relaxed beneath a fishing boat, I watched fishermen follow the trail of phosphorescent light made by the splashing sardines. A motor-powered boat circled the sardines and dropped a net with lead weights on the bottom and cork floats on top. Men on both ends of the boat pulled in the wings of the net, and the sardines formed a school and swam right into it! If those sardines only knew it, they could escape by going on a wild breakaway before the net closed, or by diving under the boat.

"To stop them, the fishermen churn the water in the gap to make more glowing 'fire' and scare those silly sardines right back into the net. I'm too strong to get trapped in those nets and too experienced to be fooled by bait with a hook inside."

"But the clever fishermen of 'California' outsmart the sardines every time," observed Calafia.

Voyaging in a Tomol

"Oh Calafia, great queen of the watery world, wise mistress of all creatures that swim below the waves, I am your servant the swordfish, shiny and swift.

"Unlike birds, the humans can't fly from the mainland to the Channel Islands. Unlike me, they cannot swim the wide ocean. But with my unblinking black eyes, I watch the Chumash men paddle and paddle their red

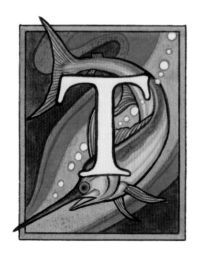

oceangoing canoe. They call it a *tomol*, and with it they travel the waters. They fish and hunt sea lions and seals. They can paddle the tomol all day long, from mainland to island.

"Their building tools are gifts from the ocean: whale ribs for splitting logs, seashells for scraping and drilling, and sharkskin for smoothing. They gather the gifts of the land for building: driftwood logs for planks, milkweed fibers to sew the planks together, and sticky pitch and tar to seal the gaps.

"On a journey, the Chumash voyagers may face a screaming storm or become lost in banks of silent fog. Sometimes migrating gray whales join them unexpectedly."

"Slippery swordfish, you would serve me better by swallowing your flattery!" scolded Calafia. "Save your praise for the ingenious Chumash builders who fashion boats without using metal."

The Fabulous Underground Gardens

"Oh tireless Queen Calafia, I am Beechey, a ground squirrel. Hear my story of the underground gardens of Baldassare Forestiere. The sun makes everything grow in our big valley. And it makes the valley hot as an oven all summer. It's much cooler underground. Forestiere used simple farm tools to dig his own little cellar home with a bedroom and kitchen. I wonder what people thought about that.

"Every ground squirrel has its own burrow entrance and so did Forestiere. Green and purple grapes shaded it, and he even carved a peephole in the door so he could see who was coming down the steps. Strawberries, kumquats, and dates flourished in his underground garden. Citrus trees grew toward openings in the earth above. He grafted one tree to bear seven kinds of fruit!

"Hardpan is a layer of soil underground, hard as iron. For forty-one years, starting in 1905, Forestiere stacked chunks of hardpan to build arches, pillars, and planters. Maybe the Roman ruins in his Sicilian homeland inspired him. Generations of curious ground squirrels watched Forestiere as he dug acres of tunnels, rooms, and passages. He never gave up on his dream of an underground garden resort."

"Your 'California' is like a garden where the creative spirit can grow," mused the queen.

27

Vaqueros: The Original Cowboys

"Oh sky-riding Queen Calafia, you will certainly admire the skills of the vaqueros. *Vaca* means 'cow' and *vaquero* means 'cowboy.' The vaqueros of early 'California' were the first cowboys.

"I am a chuckwalla, a kind of desert lizard. Once, a herd of bellowing cattle forced me to scramble up a rocky mound for safety. From my lookout I saw vaqueros on horseback, plunging through the dust and brush of the chaparral, galloping amid the flood of tossing horns.

"Do your women warriors use a lariat to lasso the ferocious griffins? Our vaqueros are masters of the lariat. I watched a vaquero fling his lariat and—like magic—the whirling loop snagged the horns of a thousand-pound steer. The vaquero expertly flicked the slack line around the 'heels' of the bull, bringing it stumbling to the ground. The vaquero must instantly dally the rope around his saddle horn; a lariat snapping taut could cut off his fingers!

"The horse knew its job and kept the lariat tight while the vaquero dismounted to secure the struggling steer. Other vaqueros moved in to brand it with the ranchero's mark, and then they turned it loose."

"Horse riders or griffin riders—they all have skills to be proud of," remarked Calafia.

The Wonderful Watts Towers

"Oh Queen Calafia, I am Tadarida, the free-tailed bat. I'm proud to speak for all the night creatures where I live, the Los Angeles neighborhood of Watts. Night is when I feed. Neon store signs, streetlights, and porch lights attract flying insects. Where they swarm into the lights, I eat my fill.

"Contrary to what many people think, bats are not blind. We see very well in the dark. One night, as I zoomed toward the brilliant beam of a big red electric trolley car, I flew into a maze of weird towers, archways, and shrines, everything decorated with broken tiles, bottle glass, seashells, and even toys. The place looked a little like a ship or a cathedral, but really, it was like nothing else I'd ever seen! In the enchantment of the night, everything in that fantasyland looked magical.

"A man called Sam Rodia built the towers out of steel bars, wire mesh, and concrete—all by himself. He'd been at it for years before I came along. I often returned at night to find him high up in one of his towers, singing while he worked. The last time I saw him there was in 1954....Why do you think he built it?"

"A true artist," said Calafia, "doesn't need a reason to create something wonderful."

Faster Than Sound: The X-1 Rocket Plane

"*Kak-kak-kak!* Hear me, oh fierce Queen Calafia. I am Falco the peregrine falcon, fastest animal on earth. Like your warriors on their griffins, I plunge from the sky to strike my prey. My deadly attacking dive is called a 'stoop.' Nothing escapes me. I can hit anything, from a hummingbird to a hawk.

"But the humans build things called airplanes that fly even faster than Falco. Airplanes are not birds. They have wings but no feathers. Their engines screech and roar.

"One morning in 1946 while I soared above the desert, a big airplane climbed past me. It carried a small plane tucked under its belly. The little plane dropped free...and then suddenly rockets burned bright in its tail and hurled it forward. The little plane shrieked away, speeding faster and faster. With my sharp eyes I was following its straight, white cloud trail when, without warning, an invisible shock wave tumbled me upside down. Just as I recovered, a noise like exploding thunder came from the rocket plane. It had broken the sound barrier. *Ka-booom!* I am faster than the wind but that airplane flew faster than sound!"

"Will the desire for speed ever be satisfied?" wondered the queen.

Adventuring in Yosemite with John Muir

"Greetings, Queen Calafia, mistress of the magic island! I am Chuck, the yellow-bellied marmot. While I sit and sun myself I often watch a bearded man named John Muir hike the meadows and gorges of Yosemite Valley. He travels alone, not in noisy groups like the other people.

"Every waterfall, plant, and animal fascinates him. I study him just as closely as he studies us. His actions are unpredictable. Would you climb a Douglas fir tree just to ride it in a windstorm? He is drawn to high ledges and sheer granite walls. He climbs cliffs soaked by waterfalls just to see their rainbows by day and, when the moon is full, 'moon-bows' by night. Once I saw him scramble behind Yosemite Falls just to gaze at the moon through what he calls 'veils' and 'comets' of falling water.

"Such risky behavior has a price! Once—it was in 1872—he was knocked unconscious when he fell and hit his head near Tenaya Falls. Another time— same year!—a snow avalanche carried him to the bottom of a canyon. I prefer my burrow to those dangers, but Muir gladly paid the price to study the secrets of this splendid valley."

Calafia said, "Nature's mysteries in your 'California' excite my curiosity."

Saved by the Zoo

"Please hear our stories, oh patient queen," implored a huge Kodiak bear. He stood with four other remarkable creatures, all silent and trembling with worry. "We weren't born in 'California.' We came from all over the world to the zoo in San Diego, so now we are 'Californians' too. My name is Caesar. After I retired as a ship's mascot from the Navy, I rode to the zoo in a car."

"Amusing," said Calafia. "Now let us hear from your companions too."

"My journey was not so fun," said the white rhinoceros. "Poachers want to kill us for our horns. I voyaged for twenty-five days from South Africa on the deck of a ship to get to 'California.' I was sick the entire trip. Now I am happy and well in the zoo's wild animal park."

"I'm a refugee from the wars in my Asian jungle," said the whiskery douc langur, "and fortunate to have a safe new home at the zoo."

"I was an orphan, just a joey in my mother's pouch when she died," said Gumdrop the Queensland koala. "The eucalyptus trees make me feel at home in 'Koalafornia.'"

"I came from China," said the Manchurian crane. "I am honored to represent my homeland—and proud to be a 'Californian!'"

"Without a doubt, these zoo animals speak for the people of 'California' as well," declared the queen.

Queen Calafia's Judgment

"Liota!" The queen's voice echoed through the royal audience chamber. "You brought five zoo animals to our island instead of just one. That makes thirty-one creatures, not the twenty-six I ordered! You rarely disappoint me...but never mind. Theirs was the final story, and we have heard all we need to hear. I am ready to deliver my judgment."

No sound came from the startled animals in the audience chamber. The ranks of warrior-women-at-arms remained rigidly at attention.

Calafia gestured sternly to the embarrassed Liota, who quickly ordered food and drinks for the animal witnesses. Speaking before the great queen had taxed their nerves and dried their tongues.

At last, Calafia spoke again. "I am grateful to every creature in this chamber and I honor you for your courtesy and sincerity. The stories you told are a credit to each of you and paint vivid portraits of your homeland.

"Your land, like mine, is a wild country where each day brings another fight for survival. The stories of the earthquake and fire, of the struggle in the tar pit, and even the life of the butterfly show how your people persevere and animals endure.

"I did not expect that magic could exist anywhere beyond my magic island, yet an uncanny magic is found throughout your land. There is the magic of the enchanting 'Jewel City,' of fantastic gardens that flourish underground, and of Hollywood's spellbinding illusions.

"The majestic giant redwood trees, the desolate grandeur of Death Valley, and the shimmer of a Yosemite moon-bow are examples of nature's lavish beauty. They are equaled only by the magnificent views on my magic island.

"I never imagined the remarkable variety of wild creatures that dwell in your land—and I reign over an island teeming with wild griffins! Flying squirrel, free-tailed bat, Gila monster...your lives are a wonderment. Each fascinating story has captivated us with its novelty.

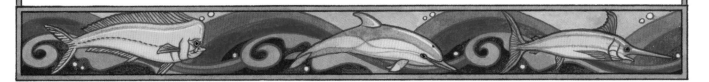

"It is unfortunate that your 'Californians' are often arrogant and inconsiderate. So many of them act foolishly, with no thought of tomorrow. Their wastefulness and desire to have control over every other creature weigh against them.

"But to be fair, I must not overlook their imagination and inventiveness. The coaches that roll on rails through mountain tunnels, the oceangoing boats made by hand, and the giant mirror that reflects all the stars are marvels unknown in my kingdom. Scientists, artists, and dreamers had their places in your stories too.

"It was the multitude of 'Californians' who do their best every day to build an ideal world, a world where people of all lands might gather to make new lives, that tipped the balance"—here the queen paused, but no one made a sound—"in their favor.

"Now I finally understand how the legends of California the Magic Island led others to confuse our two lands. The legend that my island abounds with gold is true, and I believe it was the mountains of gold in your land that sparked people to rashly claim the name of California. Nonetheless, you have proved that your land compares favorably with my magic island in every way. Our name has not been dishonored. Indeed, I am proud that a land such as yours bears the name. Let there be an end to this misunderstanding. Accept the forgiveness of a queen.

"Hear my judgment! From this day forward, all animals that dwell in your land and all the human generations yet to come shall proudly call their land 'California,' recalling the ideal world of my magic island and honoring my name. I promise I will devote myself to the people of California and watch over their land forever."

At this pronouncement, each animal cheered and applauded in its own way. Tails thumped and fins slapped. There was stamping, flapping, and whistling. The warriors stood at ease. California was spared Calafia's wrath and was now under her eternal protection.

After many good-byes and congratulations, a royal griffin and its rider escorted each creature back to its California home. Every creature was proud of its part in the drama. All of their stories would be remembered and retold forever. 🍁

If you wish to learn more about the animals, people, places, and events in these stories, you are in luck! Queen Calafia instructed her lieutenant to learn everything possible about them. Liota assembled a complete record of the animals' visit in a volume known as the Golden Ledger. The author of California, the Magic Island *studied the Golden Ledger and then added his own research to compile the following notes. The enthusiastic artist couldn't help pointing out the most interesting details included in the pictures.*

Pearls from the Golden Ledger

Queen Calafia and Her Magic Island originated with the Spanish writer Garci Rodríguez de Montalvo, who introduced the beautiful warrior-queen in a romantic adventure novel, *Las Sergas de Esplandián* (the exploits of Esplandián), over five centuries ago. The exploits begin with this arresting statement: "I tell you that on the right-hand side of the Indies there was an island called California...." This popular story established the basic elements of the California legend, including the courageous black-skinned Amazon women, the ferocious griffins, and the abundance of gold, "which was the only metal on the island."

The author of *California, the Magic Island* was inspired to create his own version of the Calafia legend, which includes details from *The Exploits of Esplandián* but ends much differently. The character of Liota, the profusion of pearls, and even the mention of the "very well-designed caves" all sparked the imagination of the artist.

Other creative individuals have admired the Calafia legend and reinterpreted it in their art and writing. Artist Maynard Dixon included the queen (and her warriors and griffins too) in a magnificent mural in San Francisco's Mark Hopkins Hotel.

In modern-day works the queen is often called *"Califia,"* perhaps because this spelling aligns more closely with that of "California."

 Wit, a California condor, recounts the story of The Doomed Explorer of Alta California. Wit is the condor of Chumash Indian myth who finds missing people and lost objects.

A nine-foot wingspan makes the condor the largest land bird in North America. Despite its fierce look, the condor is a scavenger; it cannot catch or kill its own food. The condor's bald head helps keep animal gore from sticking as it eats.

Wit's story begins in 1542 during Juan Rodríguez Cabrillo's voyage along the coast of California and ends with the voyager's death on January 3, 1543. The voyagers left Guatemala and explored the coasts of Baja and Alta California as far north as Point Reyes. One account of Cabrillo's accident says he injured his shoulder. Whether shoulder or shin, he developed gangrene and died nine days later.

Although the story of Calafia, queen of California, was published more than thirty years before Cabrillo's final voyage, the promise of gold kept the story alive. At first, the Baja California peninsula appeared to be Calafia's mythical island, but Cabrillo and others of his time probably came to realize that the island of California was just a myth. Even so, it continued to appear on maps as late as the eighteenth century.

 Dana's personal story unfolds in Journey of a Monarch Butterfly Queen. Her name comes from the monarch's scientific name, *Danaus plexippus.*

The monarch butterflies in California don't migrate to Mexico like their Canadian butterfly relations. Instead they stay west of the Rocky Mountains. Thousands cluster in groves of eucalyptus, pine, and cypress trees along the California coast. Resembling a mass of dead leaves, they rest quietly in cold weather until sunlight warms them enough to fly.

The story takes place in spring, when the female monarchs lay hundreds of pinhead-sized eggs on the undersides of milkweed leaves. Because of the larvae's diet of milkweed, the butterflies carry a bitter chemical taste that protects them from most predators. The vivid coloring of the monarch is a signal that says, "You don't want to eat me!" Can you see Dana's enemy the black-headed grosbeak flying past the distant trees? The colors of the grosbeak are the same as the monarch's: orange, black, and white.

Black-foot, a black-footed albatross, describes Chasing the *China Clipper.* These wide-ranging birds are at home on the Pacific Ocean; after they leave their breeding colony, they spend three years at sea, never touching land. They sleep on the water and possibly even in the air. "Dabbling" is the term for how albatross dip their heads below the water to grab squid and fish. Compare Black-foot's six-foot wingspan to the 130-foot span of the Martin M-130 flying boats—the *China Clippers.*

The Pan American World Airways *China Clippers* flew passengers across the Pacific from 1935 until war came to the US in 1941. Each plane could carry a dozen passengers in comfort. To fly to China, the aircraft departed from the San Francisco Bay and made overnight stops in Honolulu, Midway Island, Wake Island (where Black-foot was hatched), Guam, Manila, and finally Hong Kong!

The original China clippers were fast sailing ships that carried tea from China in the mid-1800s. They were known as clippers because they sailed "at a good clip."

The aerial view shows Yerba Buena Island and the San Francisco–Oakland Bay Bridge. Did you notice the tunnel through the island? To the left is Treasure Island, a man-made island built for the Golden Gate International Exposition in 1939. The *China Clippers* made it their home base starting in 1940.

The mustang from The Wild Horses of Death Valley didn't give his name. Maybe his long mane and dappled markings will inspire a reader to choose the perfect name for him. In the picture he is dodging a venomous Panamint rattlesnake. Oxidizing minerals created the multicolored rock formation in the background known as Artist's Palette.

The story takes place not long after the disastrous experience of the lost pioneers of 1849 who named the place Death Valley. Death Valley holds several records. Its floor is the driest place in all of North America, and the sink at Badwater is the lowest, at 282 feet below sea level. The hottest air temperature ever recorded on earth was 134°F at Furnace Creek.

In The Earthquake and the Firehouse Dog, the energetic dog pictured barking on the street is a rat terrier. This seemed appropriate to the artist because the vigorous shaking of the earthquake has been so often described as "like a terrier shaking a rat."

Foreshocks of the earthquake occurred before sunrise on April 18, 1906. The main shock and fires soon followed. Once the flames ran out of control, the fire ate up one neighborhood after another for three terrible days and nights.

Steam is shown billowing from the boiler that powered the pumping engine, but there wasn't much water available to pump because so many mains were broken—you can see one below the cracked street.

The artist was inspired by the words of writer Jack London, who witnessed the fire and described the pall of smoke as "a rose color that pulsed and fluttered with lavender shades."

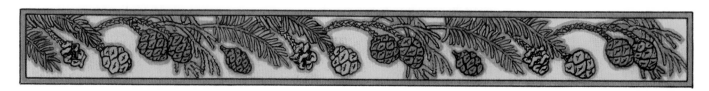

A western gull witnesses The Forty-Niners' Gold Rush Scramble. Like most gulls, it doesn't miss any opportunity to scavenge, scrounge, or steal its next meal.

The life of a sailor was difficult. Pay was meager and often delayed until the end of a voyage. Captains would anchor far offshore, afraid that if they let the men go ashore, they wouldn't return. That's just what happened when news of the discovery of gold in Sacramento reached the arriving ships. Did you notice the angry captain, shouting at the sailors who have "jumped ship"?

Photographs from that time show so many ships abandoned and rotting in the San Francisco Bay that their wooden masts look like an endless forest. Some were eventually turned into hotels or warehouses.

Strix, a northern spotted owl, narrates the tale of the Fall of the Giant Redwoods. His name comes from the scientific name of his species, *Strix occidentalis caurina*. Spotted owls are endangered because only 5 percent of their old-growth forest habitat remains.

There are two kinds of "big trees" in California. The giant sequoias in the Sierra are the thickest and most massive; the coast redwoods are the tallest. A 379-foot coast redwood named Hyperion is the world's tallest tree.

The story takes place between 1850 and 1880, during the early days of the redwood logging industry and long before the invention of gasoline engines and chain saws.

"Choppers" worked in pairs. The ideal team included one left-handed member. Here, they stand on "staging boards" driven into notches in the trunk so they can get above the tree's thick base and have room to swing their double-bitted falling axes. Below them are a man with a crosscut saw, two men chaining logs to a sturdy cart pulled by oxen, a "peeler" working to remove the redwood bark, and two men "bucking" the logs into segments.

A mealy parrot reveals the Secrets of Hollywood Movie Magic. The parrot costarred in the 1934 movie *Treasure Island*. This species is called "mealy" because its gray-green feathers appear to be dusted with a light sprinkling of flour.

The "movie magic" technology described by the parrot is typical of the early days of filmmaking. Readers probably know that special effects today are more complex and highly developed.

The flying carpet scene in the illustration is inspired by two old-time versions of *The Thief of Bagdad*. In the silent, black-and-white 1924 movie, the flying carpet was really a sheet of steel rigged by sixteen piano wires to a crane. The 1940 version was filmed in vivid Technicolor that inspired the colorful model city in the illustration. That film was the first to ever use a "blue screen" to layer a figure in the foreground against a different background.

The banded Gila monster that reports the story of The Imperial Valley and the Great Flood is one of only a few venomous lizards in the world, but no human is known to have died from its bite. The Gila monster in the story lived in the lower right-hand corner of California, right between the Colorado River and the Imperial Canal.

The disaster began in 1905 when an illegal, temporary dam bypass built just over the border in Mexico was breached by the flooding Colorado River. Photographs of the disaster show waterfalls of muddy water raging near Calexico, people in boats rowing past flooded farm buildings, and twisted railroad tracks just like in the illustration. The lake created by the great flood still exists. Look at a map to see the Salton Sea, the largest lake in California.

The star storyteller of The Glittering Tower of Jewels is a rock pigeon, also known as a rock dove. It has a recognizable head-bobbing walk and makes a clapping sound on takeoff.

The Tower of Jewels was the 435-foot-tall centerpiece of the Panama-Pacific International Exposition. It was decorated with 102,000 Novagems: faceted, cut-glass "jewels."

The exposition's name suggests that it was meant to honor the completion of the Panama Canal, which opened the year before. But to many San Franciscans, the exposition celebrated the rebirth of their city after its near destruction nine years earlier in the fire of 1906. On special occasions, ruby-colored lights and pans of red "fire" in the structure created a memorable illusion called "Burning the Tower."

Corvus, a common raven, describes what is hidden within King Sargon's Palace. The scientifc name for ravens is *Corvus corax*. Like other birds in the corvid family—crows, jays, magpies, and jackdaws—they are known for their intelligence. They are the largest of all perching birds, with a wingspan of four feet. They are mainly scavengers and eat nearly anything, including garbage and roadkill. They soar more often than crows, and they frequently walk and hop along on the ground.

Construction of the "palace" that would house the Samson Tire and Rubber Company plant began in 1929. Founder Adolph Schleicher named his company "Samson" after the famous figure from the Bible to signify the strength and endurance of his tires and of his factory. Samson's homeland was conquered by Assyria, and the Assyrian King Sargon II built a palace around 700 B.C.E. at what is now Khorsabad, Iraq. This is the palace that inspired the twentieth-century architects who designed the tire factory. When it opened in 1930, the "palace" housed the largest manufacturing facility under one roof west of the Mississippi. In 1931 Schleicher sold the company to US Tire and Rubber, which later became Uniroyal (about the same time the plant became part of the newly incorporated City of Commerce). The tire factory closed in 1978 and the refurbished palace eventually became home to an outlet mall called Citadel Outlets.

The Struggle for Survival at the La Brea Tar Pits was witnessed by the Harlan's ground sloth. The giant sloth, visible in the distance, weighed thirty-five hundred pounds and measured six feet from head to tail. It had large claws, which it likely used to dig up plant roots for food.

The story takes place twenty thousand years ago, at the end of the last ice age. The location is Rancho La Brea, in the Los Angeles Basin, where the asphalt seeps preserve a wealth of animal bones. Visitors will see the asphalt still oozing onto the streets and sidewalks today.

The Columbian mammoth was one of the largest elephants to ever live, growing up to thirteen feet tall and weighing up to ten tons. The dire wolf was the dominant carnivore of the era, preying on bison, horses, and sloths.

The Page Museum murals painted by Charles R. Knight in 1925 still excite visitors, but new research has led to changes in how paleontologists think some of the animals looked. The sabretoothed cats preferred brushy undergrowth, and so they may have been spotted like other big cats that ambush their prey. Knight painted the teratorns with the black plumage and naked heads of condor-like scavengers. However, their skeletons indicate they were ground-stalking predators, probably with light-colored, feathered heads.

A coyote tells the Tale of a Twenty-Mule Team. Popular legends portray coyotes as smart and tricky—they have to be, to survive on their own in the desert.

The coyote encounters the mule team sometime between 1883 and 1888, years when the twenty-mule teams made their longest runs, from the Harmony Borax Works in Death Valley to the railhead terminals in Daggett and Mojave. They hauled sacks of borax, a powdery white mineral used in detergent.

The wagons in the picture are some of the biggest ever made and they were built to last five years without a breakdown. The seven-foot wheels were made of hickory and their tires of iron. Each seventy-eight-hundred-pound wagon could carry a load of twenty-two thousand pounds. For the dry stretches, a water wagon was hitched in the rear.

The driver, or "teamster," controlled the team and cared for the mules. Can you guess which mule is named Milky? In some teams, the two "wheelers" were big, strong horses instead of mules. The teamster guided the mules with a "jerk line" of cotton rope going to the left leader. The other man is the "swamper." His job was to gather firewood, cook, and man the brakes.

Delphina, the short-beaked common dolphin, describes being On Maneuvers with the Navy. Her name comes from her scientific name, *Delphinus delphis*. Besides riding bow waves, dolphins engage in playful tail slapping, chin slapping, and a trick called pitch poling, where they flip end-over-end. Did you notice the crisscross or hourglass-shaped markings on Delphina's side?

In 1940 the Pacific Fleet was known as the Battle Fleet and was stationed at San Diego. Every year the sailors trained by participating in practices called "fleet problems." The warships in the picture represent the look of the US Navy a year before it was attacked at Pearl Harbor, Hawai'i. Included are the submarine USS *Sargo*, the battleship USS *California*, the light cruiser USS *Concord*, a patrol torpedo (PT) boat, and the aircraft carrier USS *Lexington*. The three amphibious aircraft flying overhead are Consolidated P2Y patrol planes.

A common poor-will remembers The Observatory and the "Big Eye." The bird is named for the sound it makes, a repeated call that sounds like "poor Will."

The "Big Eye" for the two-hundred-inch reflecting telescope was twice the diameter of any mirror cast before. It took a year to cool. A special train carried it from New York to California. It took eleven years (1936–1947), with a delay during World War II, to polish the mirror at the Caltech optics lab in Pasadena.

Palomar Mountain was chosen for the observatory site because it is a stable granite block, safe from the shaking of earthquakes and far from air and light pollution. In November 1947 Belyea Trucking was selected to move the carefully crated mirror to the mountaintop. The movers were famous for taking on big jobs; they'd hauled a ship, an oil rig, even a dead orca. The precious cargo was loaded onto a special tractor and double-gooseneck trailer rig, on a total of forty-two wheels.

The final climb up Palomar Mountain took place in sleet and rain. The convoy arrived at the observatory dome at eleven a.m., but the artist chose to show the scene at night to emphasize the stars.

Sabrina, a northern flying squirrel, relates *A Night Ride with the Pony Express.* Her scientific name is *Glaucomys sabrinus.*

In the years before the American Civil War, news from the eastern United States took weeks to reach California. A mail-delivery service called the Pony Express cut the time to as few as eight days. From 1860 to 1861, relays of tough young horsemen rode day and night from St. Joseph, Missouri, to Sacramento, California. The riders had to weigh less than 120 pounds because speed was essential to complete the 1,840-mile route on schedule.

Westbound riders crossed the Great Plains, Rocky Mountains, Great Salt Desert, and Sierra Nevada before entering California near the southern shore of Lake Tahoe. The illustration depicts Sugar Loaf Station, named for the mountain in the background.

Just eighteen months after the Pony Express was founded, the Pacific Telegraph Company completed its line to San Francisco and the Pony Express went out of business.

The Little Lost Quail is the personal story of Pillow, a California quail. The story unfolds during summer in the foothills of the Sacramento Valley, but quail live nearly everywhere in California. Perhaps that's why the California quail is the state bird.

Quail can fly when only ten days old. After hatching, several broods may mix; male and female adults cooperate and care for the young. In spring the coveys break up into pairs. Once a pair is formed, the two birds will stay with each other for the rest of the breeding season. Did you know that the plume, or topknot, on the adult quail is formed from six overlapping feathers?

The hawk in the illustration is the sharp-shinned hawk. Other winged quail predators are Cooper's hawks, great horned owls, and jays. On the ground, quails must beware of snakes, skunks, ground squirrels, coyotes, bobcats, and house cats too.

A Sierra Nevada bighorn sheep watched the men *Working on the Railroad.* Bighorn sheep have specialized hooves with hard outer edges and spongy soles to provide traction.

Two railroad companies, working from opposite sides of the country, raced to lay track and eventually connect in one transcontinental railroad. The illustration shows a triumphant moment in August 1867 when the Central Pacific Railroad finished the Summit Tunnel near Donner Pass. A wood-burning locomotive chugs past the Chinese laborers who performed most of the work on the tunnel. Tunneling through solid granite involved drilling, chiseling, and blasting—often gaining only a foot each day. Individuals worked six twelve-hour days a week.

To express the scope of the rail builders' achievements, the artist combined the portal of the Summit Tunnel with a panoramic view of the American River Valley as seen from a tight curve the railroad men named Cape Horn.

The railroad provided a monotonous diet of beef, beans, bread, butter, and potatoes for the Caucasian workers, many of them Irish. The Chinese had to pay for their food but enjoyed remarkable variety. Their grocery list included fresh vegetables, pork, poultry, salted cabbage, dried fruit, rice, dried oysters, seaweed, and bamboo sprouts. Instead of water the Chinese drank tea, which proved to be more healthful.

Cory the mahi-mahi shares some Secrets of Sardine Fishing. He is a dolphin fish (scientific name *Coryphaena hippurus*), but don't confuse him with a common dolphin, which is definitely *not a fish*. Like us humans, it is a mammal.

The year is 1929, during the heyday of the sardine industry. The fishing crews were mostly Italian and Sicilian. They made their catch in the waters off Monterey, then delivered the fish right to the cannery.

Fishermen chose moonless nights to follow the fiery luminescence stirred up by the movement of the sardines through the water. The artist has pictured a team of men at the bow and stern of the boat, racing each other to haul in the wings of the net. The net can hold many tons of fish. To keep the sardines from escaping through the gap, one man uses a "scare" to churn up the luminescent "fire." The scare is a rope with a weight on the bottom and small wooden paddles attached every six feet or so.

The jellyfish in the picture are of the type sometimes called the crystal jelly, and they glow with their own light.

A swordfish recounts the tale about Voyaging in a Tomol. Swordfish are venerated animals in Chumash culture, believed to be the ocean's equivalent of human beings. The scientific name for swordfish is *Xiphias gladius*. Did you know the gladius was a sword used by Roman foot soldiers?

Pods of migrating gray whales can be identified by their heart-shaped spouts, or "blows." In the illustration, the whitish patches on the whales are barnacles. The barnacles don't hurt the whales. Brown pelicans fly in staggered formation along the horizon.

The setting is the Chumash Indian homeland, which included the coast between Malibu and Paso Robles and the three northern Channel Islands. It took real skill and knowledge to construct a *tomol*, and the members of the Brotherhood of the Tomol held respected places in Chumash society.

The word for the sticky caulking made of sap and tar is *yop*. The milkweed-fiber stitching that held the boat's planks together was painted with the black yop, making a distinctive pattern. In the picture, one man is baling water with an abalone shell, and abalone shell fragments decorate the boat's bow. There are no seats in the tomol; the men kneel on tule knee mats to paddle.

A California ground squirrel tells the story of The Fabulous Underground Gardens. The author's name for this squirrel, "Beechey," comes from its scientific name, *Otospermophilus beecheyi*. In the picture, lookouts can be seen standing on their hind legs with clasped paws. Their metallic, chirping call warns nearby squirrels of the approach of predators.

The story takes place between 1905, when Forestiere bought his eighty acres, and 1946, when he died. Before moving to California, he worked as a subway digger in Boston, Massachusetts. That could be where he first learned his tunneling skills. The gardens are in Fresno, in the central San Joaquin Valley. It's a locale well known for foggy winters and blazing summers with stretches of days over 100 or even 110 degrees.

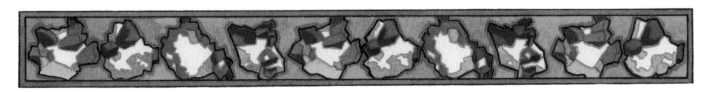

A common chuckwalla introduces Calafia to the Vaqueros: The Original Cowboys.

To resist predators, a chuckwalla wedges itself into a crevice and inflates its body. The Cahuilla Indians pulled the chuckwallas from their crevices with special sticks.

Long-horned cattle go back centuries, to the Iberian cattle brought by the Spanish settlers of Mexico. Our vaquero story begins in the 1820s, when Mexico broke away from Spain and took over the missions, and the herds of mission cattle ended up in the hands of *rancheros*, the first cattle barons. The gold boom of the 1850s created a demand for beef—and for vaqueros, who were free to work on the ranchos or hire out for cattle drives.

Paintings and engravings from that time record the kind of colorful attire seen in this illustration. Silver decorations might appear on bridles, saddles, hats, and trousers, depending on the wealth of the vaquero.

The vocabulary of the vaqueros evolved into that of the cowboy: the braided rope, *la reata*, became "lariat"; the heavy leather trousers, *chaparreras*, became "chaps." The American cowboys even changed *vaquero* to "buckaroo"!

Construction of The Wonderful Watts Towers was witnessed by Tadarida, a Brazilian (or Mexican) free-tailed bat, scientific name *Tadarida brasiliensis*. A tail somewhat like what you would see on a mouse explains the "free-tailed" part of its name. Contrary to what you may have heard, bats don't need to live in caves: in the city they live in all sorts of buildings and under bridges.

Sam Rodia was born in Italy as Sabato Rodia, and he was known by a variety of names, including Don Simon, Simon Rodilla, and Sam. He was a master concrete finisher and used all of his free time from 1921 to 1954 (thirty-three years) to build the collection of towers he named *Nuestro Pueblo*, meaning "Our Town." He drew no plans, improvising as he went along. The tallest tower reaches nearly a hundred feet in height.

It's possible that Rodia chose the triangular parcel of land in Watts because it was close to the tracks from which countless train and trolley passengers could view his work.

Falco the peregrine falcon encounters an aircraft Faster Than Sound: The X-1 Rocket Plane. *Falco peregrinus* is his scientific name. Peregrine falcons are known throughout the world but encountered only rarely above Edwards Air Force Base. Specialized body parts allow the falcon to see and breathe at their diving speed of 200 miles per hour or more.

In 1947 US Air Force test pilot Capt. Charles Elwood "Chuck" Yeager pushed his Bell X-1 to 700 miles per hour (Mach 1.06). Aircraft designers had worked for years to design a plane that could "break the sound barrier," and this was the first manned aircraft to go supersonic in level flight. Yeager named the aircraft *Glamorous Glennis*, after his wife. The fuselage design was based on the shape of a conventional .50 caliber bullet.

The X-1 was launched from a modified B-29 carrier aircraft before achieving its speed record. The record-setting flight took place above Muroc Dry Lake. Muroc Army Air Base was used for secret testing that also included the famous X-15. (X stands for "experimental.") The base was renamed Edwards Air Force Base in 1950. In later decades NASA's space shuttles landed at Edwards eighteen times.

 Chuck, a yellow-bellied marmot, recalls *Adventuring in Yosemite with John Muir*. The marmot is also known as the "rock chuck," and that's where our narrator gets his name. The marmot is a kind of ground squirrel but not very energetic. When he isn't hibernating, his preferred activity is grooming himself and lying in the sun. Modern-day marmots are notorious in Yosemite for munching on boots, backpacks, and the rubber radiator hoses of parked automobiles.

The artwork illustrates a lunar spray-bow, or moon-bow, at the base of Yosemite Falls. In 1868 John Muir observed spray-bows at the foot of the Upper Yosemite Fall and farther up, at Fern Ledge.

Muir was vital to the establishment of Yosemite as a national park in 1890. Later, a private camping trip with President Theodore Roosevelt seems to have ensured that Yosemite Valley and the Mariposa Grove would also become part of the park, in 1906. Muir cofounded the Sierra Club and embodied its mission, "To explore, enjoy, and protect the wild places of the earth."

 Caesar the Kodiak bear was the first of the five animals in the story to be *Saved by the Zoo*. It turns out that the sailors on the USS *Nanshan* who adopted Caesar for a mascot didn't know much about bears—Caesar was a female. She is shown in 1916 riding with Dr. Joseph "Snake" Thompson, a herpetologist and a founder of the San Diego Zoological Society.

The southern white rhinoceros arrived at the zoo in 1970 with eighteen other survivors. They had been driven by truck from a game preserve in Zululand to Durban, South Africa, and then spent twenty-five days on the deck of a freighter to Galveston, Texas, before traveling by train to San Diego.

The endangered red-shanked douc langurs arrived in 1968 from Indochina. Visitors see little of these Old World monkeys, as they prefer private areas away from view.

The zookeepers reared Gumdrop by hand when she arrived in 1977.

The rare crane was one of two that were gifts from the Peking Zoo in 1981. Manchurian cranes, also known as Japanese cranes or red-crowned cranes, are beloved symbols of love and long life; ironically, they are endangered.

The San Diego Zoo began with a handful of animals abandoned after San Diego's 1915 Panama-California Exposition and has grown ever since. Now the zoo is home to 3,700 animals of more than 650 species and subspecies.

The borders at the beginning of this book are decorated with rocks, minerals, and gemstones found in California. The red stone on the first page is garnet and the other is pink tourmaline. The crescent moon is mother-of-pearl. Below are two griffin feathers with a baroque pearl suspended between them.

On the title page, starting from the upper left and going clockwise, the big decorative stones are kunzite, lepidolite, fire agate, Chinese writing rock, Morgan Hill poppy jasper, and jade.

Wild animals and plants and another mineral, all specially recognized as official state symbols, inspired other decorative borders. Starting from the dedication page at the front of the book, they are: gray whale, state marine mammal; and garibaldi, state marine fish. Beginning on page 35 are the California grizzly bear, state animal; cones and needles of the coast redwood and sequoia, state trees; California dogface butterfly, state insect; purple needlegrass, state grass; desert tortoise, state reptile; golden trout, state freshwater fish; benitoite, state gemstone; and California quail, state bird. The border on this page is the California poppy, state flower.

The five other borders contain California-dwelling birds, fish, mammals, and a reptile already described in the stories, as well as other plants found in the state. The border below Calafia's portrait includes almond blossoms, olives, an orange, grapes, an avocado, an artichoke, a fig, and cherries, all rendered as jewels. The border below the stormy Magic Island also depicts its subjects as jewels. They include a cocklebur, mesquite thorns, a rattlesnake, a prickly pear cactus, and a thistle.

About the Author

Doug Hansen is the eldest of six children in an artistic family. He was born in Fresno, California, and has lived and worked there since 1970. Doug is a professor of illustration at California State University, Fresno, in the Department of Art and Design and was a newsroom artist at *The Fresno Bee* for twenty-two years. In addition to *California, the Magic Island*, he has authored two other children's books published by Heyday, *Mother Goose in California* and *Aesop in California*.

Acknowledgments

Writing and illustrating a book requires faith. I have to believe the ideas and words and pictures will come to life in my brain and then on paper when I need them, and my publisher must have faith in me as a creative artist. To my immense satisfaction, Heyday has trusted me to find another perspective on the California-centric children's book, and the result is *California, the Magic Island.*

Publisher Malcolm Margolin opened the door to our third children's book together. It was he who proposed an ABC book and brought the legend of Calafia to my attention. Through his supportive correspondence, Malcolm masterfully nurtures the relationship between artist and publisher.

I remember an early brainstorming discussion with Heyday's creative staff assembled around a very big table. Development director Marilee Enge, editorial director Gayle Wattawa, and events and outreach coordinator Lillian Fleer, among others, were involved in the discussion of my embryonic book proposal. This discussion provided a critical impetus that led to my scheme for the book's structure. Hopefully, the twenty-six otherwise disparate stories have been enriched and given unity by the need to tell them to a queen.

It continues to be a pleasure to be teamed with editor Jeannine Gendar. Her encouragement is invaluable and her empathetic collaboration is not only painless but a joyful experience that I relish. She is so fluent in all things California that not only did she identify the narrowleaf milkweed in the butterfly illustration, she acknowledged it as her favorite milkweed. What other editor can make that claim?

Without a doubt Heyday makes beautiful books. Art director Diane Lee aids, abets, and surpasses my design conceits in every way, and her knowledge and experience make our book dreams a reality. Her background in illustration strengthens our special working relationship and her unstinting enthusiasm keeps my spirits high during the years required to put together a new book.

The grace and clarity of this book, its elegant layout, and its decorative consistency are due to the ability of designer Ashley Ingram. Like everyone I've worked with at Heyday, she is a sympathetic collaborator who contributes unstintingly to creating the best book possible.

This is a good time to offer my appreciation to finance director David Isaacson, who is the gentleman responsible for detailing my book sales and sending welcome royalty checks, and to operations manager Anna Pritt, who, while efficiently following through with all of my book orders, still made time to share a candid photo of her son reading my book *Mother Goose in California.*

Finally, I express my grateful affection for Susan, my wife, who realizes that each new book requires months and years of my time in the studio. I acknowledge the scores of things deferred to that elusive day "when I finish the book." For understanding your husband-artist, I thank you.

Doug Hansen

THE MAGIC ISLAND OF CALIFORNIA